For Mum, who loves cats,
and for Dad, who is allergic – A.S.

A TEMPLAR BOOK

First published in the UK in 2012 by Templar Publishing,
an imprint of The Templar Company Limited,
The Granary, North Street, Dorking, Surrey, RH4 1DN, UK
www.templarco.co.uk

First edition

ISBN 978-1-84877-570-1

Edited by Libby Hamilton

Printed in China

Naughty Kitty!

by Adam Stower

templar publishing

Lily wanted a doggy,

but her mum said dogs were too messy,

too smelly, and far too much trouble.

So she got Lily something else...

He was a bit scruffy…
and no good at tricks…

but otherwise he
was quite cute,

especially when you
tickled his tummy.

And Mum was right,
he wasn't any trouble at all...
at first.

But then, just for a moment,

Lily left him alone...

It was a catastrophe.

What a mess!

Lily couldn't understand it.

How could you?
Eight fish fingers, all the sticky biscuits,
plums, pickles, Mum's pink party cake,
Dad's pork chop, the orange pop, two teaspoons
and a washing up sponge!

And she'd just fed him
a whole bowl of Kittibix!

Lily told Kitty to sit still
until she'd finished tidying the kitchen.
There was to be no messing, no mischief
and absolutely no scratching.

Lily was getting cross.

Surely Kitty couldn't cause any more trouble?

But by teatime things had gone from bad to worse.

and I still don't know how
you pinched **all my sausages!**

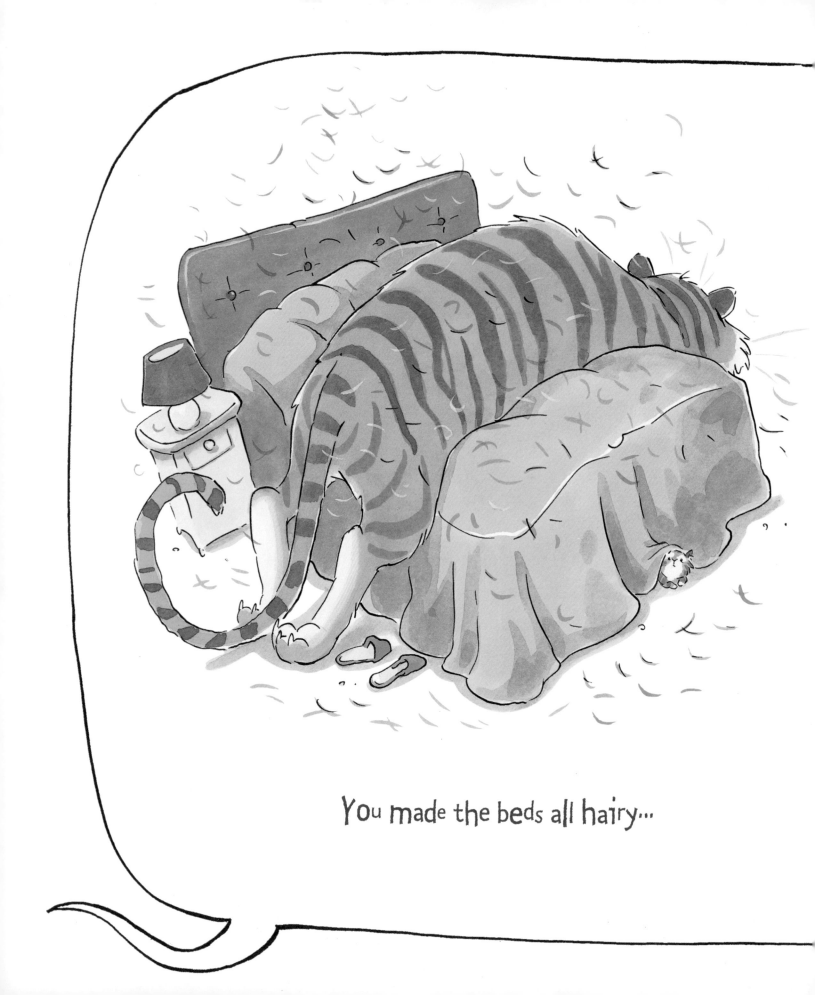

You made the beds all hairy...

and as for Mum's rug –
I can't even talk about that.
It was REVOLTING!

But just then they heard a long, low

GRRRROOOWWWWWWL!

There was something in the garden.

Something with teeth…

something with claws…

something with STRIPES!

It was Pat, the dog from next door.

Lily yelled!

Kitty YOWLED…

...and the bad dog ran away.

Perhaps Kitty wasn't so bad after all.

In fact, Lily decided he was completely fantastic

and he deserved a whole box of Kittibix,

a tummy rub and a quiet, cosy snuggle on the sofa.

So that's just what they did.